Stop!

Before you turn the page
Take a piece of paper.
Pick up your pencil.
Draw a big triangle.

At the top point of the triangle write, **Secret Government UFO Test Base.** At the left point write **Dinosaur Graveyard.** At the right point, **Humongous Horror Movie Studios.** And in the exact center of the triangle write, **Grover's Mill.**

Ah, Grover's Mill. A perfectly normal town, bustling with shops, gas stations, motels, restaurants, and schools. A small town with a great big heart, nestled snugly in the midst of —

Wait! Did we say *normal*? A studio where they film the cheapest horror movies ever made? The world's largest and smelliest graveyard of ancient dinosaur bones? A secret army base filled with captured alien spacecraft?

All this makes poor Grover's Mill the exact center of supreme intergalactic weirdness!

Turn the page.
If you dare.
Enter The Weird Zone!

ATTACK OF THE ALIEN MOLE INVADERS!

There are more books about

THE WEIRD ZONE

#1 Zombie Surf Commandos From Mars!

#2 The Incredible Shrinking Kid!

#3 The Beast From Beneath the Cafeteria!

#4 Attack of the Alien Mole Invaders!

coming to a bookstore near you . . .
#5 The Brain That Wouldn't Obey!

THE WEIRD ZONE

ATTACK OF THE ALIEN MOLE INVADERS!

by Tony Abbott

Cover illustration by Broeck Steadman
Illustrated by Lori Savastano

A
LITTLE APPLE
PAPERBACK

ST. MARY'S SCHOOL
CLYDE, OHIO

SCHOLASTIC INC.
New York Toronto London Auckland Sydney

P-2193

ISBN 0-590-67436-6

12 11 10 9 8 7 6 5 4 3 2 1   6 7 8 9/9 0 1/0

Printed in the U.S.A   40

First Scholastic printing, November 1996

For Ernest and Louise,
steadfast through the years

Contents

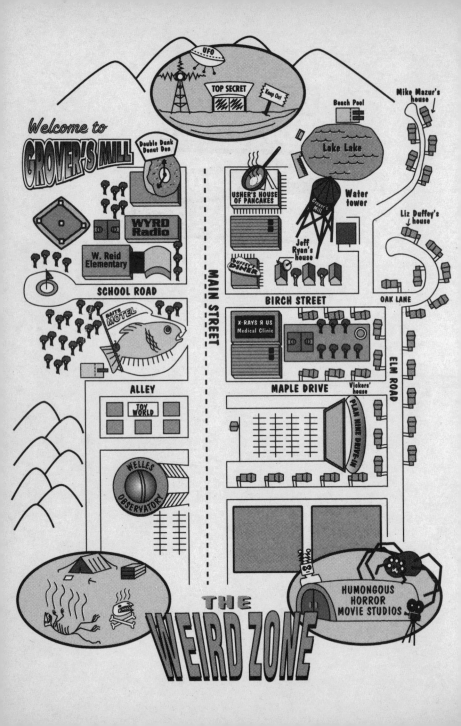

The Zoney Zone

*T*HONKA-THONKA-THONKA!

Jeff Ryan stepped back from the swishing blades of the big helicopter taking off from his front yard.

"I'm off to the shoe store, dear!" yelled Jeff's mother, swinging from a rope ladder above him.

Jeff glanced up and down Birch Street. It was a beautiful sunny Saturday. Other moms might be flipping pancakes or reading the morning newspaper.

Not his mom. She was off to her job at the shoe store.

Thonka-thonka.

A moment later, the chopper roared

away toward the hills north of Grover's Mill.

Shoe store? Jeff thought to himself. His mother had been saying that for as long as he could remember. But his friends told him there was a secret army base in those hills. A base filled with stuff captured from alien spaceships!

His friends all thought that was very weird.

Jeff sighed to himself. "But Mom would tell me the truth, wouldn't she?"

Bong! The giant donut-shaped clock on the Double Dunk Donut Den chimed the hour.

Sssss! A big puff of steam rose from the oversized pan on the top of Usher's House of Pancakes.

Grover's Mill had not one, but two giant food signs on Main Street.

His friends thought that was also very weird.

Jeff thought it was kind of funny.

"Time to go," he told himself. Jeff was

meeting his friends at Mike Mazur's house to play some street hockey. Mike's street had just been paved and it would be perfect for a game.

Jeff looked down at his skates. They were not in the best shape. They were old and getting older and tighter by the minute. And hockey wasn't really his game. He'd be lucky if he got anywhere near the puck.

Jeff curled the brim of his baseball cap, grabbed his hockey stick, and pushed off down the sidewalk.

Actually, the sidewalk sort of pushed up at him!

"Ooof!" Jeff stumbled, skidded, and landed on his face.

He turned his head — ouch! — and saw the problem. A big round bump ran across the sidewalk. In fact, it went completely across the street and up a yard on the other side.

"My lawn!" shrieked a voice from across the street. Jeff craned his neck to see

Mr. Sweeney, the janitor of W. Reid Elementary, batting furiously at the bump in his yard with a shovel.

"Uh, do you like it down there, or do you want help?" said a voice.

Jeff looked up. Holly Vickers was standing over him. She was wearing skates, too, had a hockey stick over her shoulder, and a bubble gum bubble growing slowly out of her mouth.

Holly was in Jeff's class at W. Reid Elementary. She was also the sister of his best friend Sean.

Pop! went the bubble. Holly reached down and pulled Jeff to his feet. "Weird," she said. "This street is looking more and more like a crinkle-cut french fry."

Jeff shrugged, twisting his baseball cap. "Yeah, this bump just suddenly appeared and — "

BLAMMO! The ground thundered!

Jeff dived back to the sidewalk — and this time Holly joined him — as a big, heavy manhole cover shot up from the

street next to them! It arced like a basketball going for the net and landed across the street.

CRUNNNNCH!

"My mailbox!" screamed Mr. Sweeney.

The two kids crawled slowly over to the hole in the street and looked down.

"Red," said Jeff, squinting into the sewer. "Reddish light. Do you see that?"

"Very weird, Jeff. Very zoney," Holly said. "Let's get to Mike's before the sky falls down."

"Or the street falls up!" said Jeff, grabbing his stick and twisting his cap around. "But listen, I just want you to know. Hockey isn't really my game."

"Yeah, I know, but hurry up, anyway. It's going to be fun," said Holly, already skating down the street.

"Yeah, lots of fun," Jeff mumbled, his toes starting to ache in his skates.

Two minutes later, they rolled down Cedar Circle. Mike was in front of his house. He was swatting a round black puck around with his stick. Liz Duffey sat on the curb, strapping on her Rollerblades.

"Where's Sean?" asked Jeff.

Splat! Splort! Splut! Strange slopping sounds came squishing down the street!

Everyone turned.

Suddenly, there was Sean Vickers skating up the sidewalk, soaking wet.

Holly snickered. "What happened to you?"

"A fire hydrant happened to me!" said Sean, splashing and dripping over to the curb. "I thought I heard a fire hydrant say something to me. It sounded like, 'Grok!' "

"What does 'Grok' mean?" asked Jeff.

"That's just what I asked the hydrant!" said Sean. "But when I leaned over for the answer — it blew up in my face. You should've heard Mr. Sweeney when the water flooded his lawn!"

"Whoa, just like the manhole!" said Jeff,

shooting a look at Holly. "This is getting to be a dangerous place!"

"It's not getting to be," said Liz. "It is. And it's not dangerous, it's weird. It's also not a place, it's a zone. Add it all up, you get The Weird Zone!"

Holly made a face. "Whatever," she said. "Let's play already."

Whack! Before anyone could do anything, Sean slapped the puck hard with his stick and it skidded out to the center of the street.

"Ha!" he cried, splashing after it.

"Get it!" Holly snarled and took off. Liz and Mike skated after her, but Sean got to the puck first. He shot the puck back to Jeff.

Jeff crouched low, drew his stick back, and swung down fast.

THWONK! The puck shot to the curb, skipped high, soared, and slammed against the front door of a pretty blue house across the street.

"It's not baseball, Jeff!" said Liz.

Everybody stopped skating. There was a big black streak across the front door.

"Oh, man!" said Jeff, sliding to a stop. "This is definitely *not* my game!"

"I think new people live there," said Mike. "No one's met them yet. They'll probably be okay about it."

"Yeah, sure," Jeff muttered. He hopped the curb and skated up the walk. As he got closer to the house, he saw that all the shades were down.

Maybe no one's home.

But just as Jeff climbed the front steps, the front door cracked open a little bit. It was dark inside the house.

"What do you want?" a low voice growled out of the shadows. A strange smell wafted out of the house. Like fresh dirt, Jeff thought.

From the shadows, Jeff could see a pair of small, almost reddish eyes dart here and there, as if they were looking at him from head to toe.

"Um . . . hi," said Jeff. "Our hockey puck

hit your door. We'll be more careful so that we don't — "

Before he could say another word, a dark hand jerked out of the shadows, grabbed the puck from the step, and pulled it into the house.

WHAM! The door slammed in Jeff's face.

Easy Come, Easy Go

Everyone stared at the front door of the pretty blue house. Their eyes were fixed on the spot where the puck used to be.

"Hey! What just happened?" cried Holly. "Our puck is gone!"

Jeff turned and skated back down the walk. "Why would they take our puck?"

"Ha!" sniffed Liz. "Because this is Grover's Mill, and that's the kind of weird and zoney people that live here?"

"Sounds good to me," said Mike.

"Yeah," said Sean. "I'm convinced."

Holly frowned. "I think the guy was wearing something on his face. A mask, like this." She stretched out her fingers and then brought the tips together and held them in front of her face.

"Nice," said Sean. "Looks good on you."

"I think we should ask for our puck back. Right now," said Liz, taking control.

Jeff gulped, thinking again of the odd reddish glow from the shadows. And that smell of dirt.

The five kids charged right up the front walk of the pretty blue house. Jeff tapped on the door. It creaked and swung open. "Hello?" said Jeff, not really wanting an answer.

No answer.

"They've got to be here." Sean pushed on the door and the five kids stepped into the house.

"Don't they have any lights?" said Mike, nearly stumbling in the darkness.

"Lights? What about furniture?" said Liz. "These rooms are completely empty!"

"Well, except for the dirt," said Holly, moving into the living room. "I mean, the mud is so thick you could sit on it!"

Thick, slimy mud streaked the floors. And mounds of rocks and wet dirt were piled up in the corners of what was supposed to be the dining room.

"Nice outdoorsy style," said Liz. "Let's hike back to the kitchen."

The kids stepped slowly through the rooms until they came to the cellar door. The mud on the floor was even thicker there, and wetter.

"This is pretty spooky," muttered Jeff.

"The mess," said Sean. "It's coming from down there. From the basement."

Suddenly — *Thump! Thump! Thump!*

"What was that?" gasped Jeff.

Too late. The cellar door burst open and a horde of towering shapes stormed after the kids!

"Check-out time!" screamed Liz.

The figures wore long hooded robes. Their faces were hidden. But their eyes glowed. Red.

And they were grunting! "Grok!"

"That word!" yelled Sean. "I think it means — something not good!" He skated into the living room, leaping over a low pile of rocks.

"Everybody back to my house!" cried Mike. "Except you guys with the hoods!"

That sounded good to Jeff. He bolted for the front door, as if he were sliding for third and the shortstop was inches from tagging him out. Baseball was really his game.

But the hooded shapes were everywhere! Suddenly — "Help!"

It was Holly! Her skates spun out on the mud and the hooded men rushed at her. Before Jeff could think twice, he dived over next to Holly and began to kick at the men in hoods.

The wheels on his skates were spinning!

"Grok!" the hooded men grunted.

"Get away from us, you, you, guys!" screamed Holly, swatting at their hooded heads.

Thump! Thump! Thump!

The next instant Holly and Jeff were alone in the room. They heard stamping and stomping from down below. The cellar.

Jeff's heart was pounding. He was trying to catch his breath. Holly was breathing hard, too.

"We're alone," gasped Jeff.

"Liz? Sean? Mike?" cried Holly. The rooms echoed. No answer.

Holly turned to Jeff, her eyes wide with fear. "Where did everyone go?"

Jeff looked out the window. Sunny Saturday morning. A few minutes ago they were all playing street hockey. Now this. He shook his head. "This can't be happening."

"I know," said Holly, taking a deep breath. "It's totally crazy. But still, did you see their eyes? Little red dots. Like something from one of my dad's movies."

Jeff thought of her father's movies. Todd Vickers, horror moviemaker, owner of Humongous Horror Studios. Jeff wished this were just a movie. But something told him it wasn't. It was real.

Holly turned to him. "They're aliens, Jeff. I know it!"

Whoa! he thought. *Sure, zombies from Mars had attacked Grover's Mill once, but that was weeks ago!*

Holly pointed to the back of the house. "Come on. There's only one way to find out what's going on. We have to go down there. Into the cellar."

The two kids stepped slowly downstairs, trying to make as little noise as possible with their skates.

The cellar below was divided into two rooms. One was supposed to be the playroom, the other was the room with the furnace and stuff.

Rocks were piled up high against the walls there, too.

A faint red light shone under the far door.

Jeff and Holly rolled quietly across the room.

Then they heard sounds.

Voices, low and grumbling.

Suddenly, the door swung open.

Errrk!

And they weren't alone!

Trapped!

The two kids squeezed flat in the shadows behind the door. They held their breaths.

"Our work is nearly complete, Commander Exetor!" growled a low voice.

"Mighty Zoll will be pleased," answered another voice. "This planet will soon be ours!"

Holly clutched at Jeff's arm tight. He nearly winced with pain. They both peeked around the door. Five hooded figures stood in the middle of the cellar.

They all wore long robes, almost like bathrobes, but different! And some kind of shiny silver things hung from their belts.

Tiny red eyes burned from deep beneath their hoods.

They do look like movie aliens, thought Jeff. *Maybe Holly was right.*

"And what of the earthlings, Commander Exetor?" snorted another creature.

Jeff swallowed hard. *Earthlings?* Well, that did it. If he'd learned one thing from Mr. Vickers' horror movies it was that earthlings don't call other earthlings *earthlings!*

He turned to Holly. "You're right," he whispered. "They're . . . not from around here!"

Holly swallowed, too. She formed a word with her lips. "Aliens!"

Yes, that was the word Jeff was thinking of, too.

Then, in the flickering red light, the one called Exetor removed his hood. Holly nearly choked into Jeff's shoulder. "The nose!"

Jeff gulped, trying to keep down his breakfast.

The nose. It was more like a snout. Long and thick like a pig's. But the really gross part was at the end of it. Little whiskers twitched in the air.

Holly moaned. She did that thing with her fingers on her face. "Uggg-ly, with a capital Ug!"

Jeff nodded. "They look like moles. Mole aliens."

"Ugly mole aliens," Holly whispered. "Don't forget ugly."

Jeff nodded again.

Exetor gave some kind of command and three of the moles disappeared into the shadows.

A moment later they returned, each pushing a giant glass tube to the center of the room.

The tubes stood about six feet high and three feet wide. They glowed with bluish light.

Jeff stared in horror and began to shake. He grabbed Holly's arm.

"Oh my gosh!" gasped Holly.

In the glow, standing upright, one in each tube, were . . . Liz, Sean, and Mike! They were straining to get out of the tubes.

"Sleep tight!" snorted Exetor. He pushed buttons on the outside of the tubes. An instant later, a pink gas filled the tubes and the three kids stopped moving.

"Jeff!" Holly hissed. "They can't do this!"

"Wait!" Jeff whispered. "We can't help them if we're captured, too." He held her back.

Exetor stepped over to a shiny square plate on the wall. He pushed his face against it so that his snout touched it.

Eeeee! The plate turned blue, and a panel in the floor opened up, revealing a set of glowing stairs beneath. Red light flooded into the room from below.

Exetor raised his giant hands into the air. "No one will stop the mighty Zoll! Zoll shall soon be here! Mighty Zoll will control this planet!"

VLORRRT! A second later, the three tubes carrying Liz, Mike, and Sean lowered through the floor of the cellar and disappeared.

The creatures snorted and followed them.

The floor closed up.

The cellar was empty.

Their friends were gone!

Holly jumped out of the shadows to the middle of the floor and stomped up and down on it. "Liz! Sean! Mike!" she cried out.

Clang! Clang! The floor rang under her skates as if it were made of iron. The sound died away and then there was nothing.

"Jeff," she said finally, "this is getting way too weird. We need to get some help right now!"

He shook his head. "I can't believe it. They're like . . . like . . . aliens!"

"They're not *like* aliens, Jeff, they *are*

aliens!" Holly began stomping around the room.

Jeff thought about the tiny red eyes. He nodded. "Real aliens. They said *earthlings*."

"That's it!" cried Holly, stopping and grabbing him by the arms. "Your mom must know what to do! She specializes in crazy alien stuff like this. We're going to the hills, Jeff. To the secret base where your mother works!"

Jeff looked at Holly. "Shoe store," he said quietly.

Holly rolled her eyes and pulled him along. "Yeah, but still, Jeff. Don't be surprised at what we find up there."

A second later, they were skating fast down Mike's street. At the corner they saw a tall man, looking down at something in his hands.

"It's Mr. Bell! We can tell him!" Holly screeched to a stop next to the principal of W. Reid Elementary. He was dressed in a dark suit, even though it was a warm Saturday and there was no school.

"Our friends have been abducted!" cried Jeff.

The principal looked up from the book he was reading, which was called *From Principal to President*. He smiled. *"Abducted?* I can see you've been studying your vocabulary, young man. That's a bonus word, if I'm not mistaken."

Jeff frowned. "Yes, Mr. Bell, but — "

"But, nothing!" Mr. Bell put his hands on his hips and looked down at Jeff. "I can see you're heading for a bright, shiny *A* on your report card!"

"Really?" said Jeff.

"Our friends, Mr. Bell!" sputtered Holly. "Our friends have — "

"Words are our friends, Miss Vickers!" Mr. Bell interrupted, gazing toward the mountains in the distance. "Companions, playmates, chums, pals. Ah, the good clean fun of words!" Principal Bell chuckled to

himself and strode off, his nose buried once again in his book.

"Much help?" said Holly, glaring at Mr. Bell's back. "I don't think so."

"Straight up Main Street," Jeff cried, pointing. "Then into the hills, to the shoe store."

As they tore under the huge Grover's Mill water tower, and out by Usher's House of Pancakes onto Main Street, the two kids nearly knocked down a woman carrying a stack of videos.

"Mom!" cried Holly to her mother. "Aliens!" she blurted out. "Aliens have taken Sean!"

Mrs. Vickers looked concerned. "Our Sean?"

"Yes, Mrs. V.!" said Jeff, nearly shouting. "Aliens took him underground with our other friends. Down there in the dirt."

Mrs. Vickers looked at the ground. "Oh, I'm sure he'll be all right, dear. I mean, you know Sean. He loves to get dirty."

"Well, yeah . . ." Jeff had to admit.

Holly practically exploded. "But, Mom! You don't understand! There's some kind of huge alien invasion happening in Grover's Mill. And they already have Sean! And Liz and Mike, too!"

"Aliens?" said Mrs. Vickers. "But dear, you know what I've always told you. You must ask your father. He's the alien man." The woman paused. "Oh! That came out funny, didn't it? But we love your father, don't we, dear?"

"And Sean too!" said Holly, storming off and pulling Jeff with her. "This is nuts. I mean, what's with these people? It's like they're . . ."

"Zoners?" Jeff offered, skating alongside. Zoners was the word Holly and Liz used to describe the weird people that lived in Grover's Mill.

A chilling wind swept in suddenly, and the air turned colder.

Holly looked at the clouds gathering on the horizon. Big dark rain clouds. "Yeah, Zoners. Let's keep going."

The two kids charged straight up Main Street, climbing higher and higher into the hills.

"Hurry, Jeff," urged Holly.

"Oh, man!" he grunted. "Climbing in these skates is not the easiest, you know, and besides that they're like two sizes too small and — "

"Jeff! Look!" said Holly. She pointed to a long wire fence that cut across the hills in front of them. "Looks like somebody has something to hide," she said.

"Maybe," said Jeff. "Let's check it out anyway." The two kids crept up to the fence, keeping their heads low. When they got closer they saw lights flashing behind the fence.

Guard towers loomed up just beyond the fence. Bright beacons were scanning back and forth across the ground. "Hmm," Jeff mumbled. "Lots of protection for just a shoe store."

Bong! The donut-shaped Donut Den clock chimed the hour.

Sssss! A giant puff of steam rose softly from the pan on the top of Usher's House of Pancakes.

"Time is running out," Holly said. "Let's hurry." She looked down at Grover's Mill. A storm was sweeping in as the sky darkened.

Jeff felt a lump move up his throat. "We'll find my mom and go straight back. We'll save our friends."

But what happened next shocked them.

KRAKKK! KA-RAKKK!

Jagged bolts of lightning shot from one big cloud to all the smaller ones. Suddenly, the clouds all changed direction at once. They all went left. Then they all went right.

Then they all headed for Grover's Mill.

"That's no storm," cried Jeff. "It's them! The alien invaders!"

Into the Fortress!

The two kids raced along the wire fence until they came to a gate. A heavily armed guard in a military uniform stood in front of the gate.

He stared straight ahead.

"Excuse me, sir," said Jeff. "I need to see my mother. She works here. Her name is — "

"There is no one named General Margaret P. Ryan here," the soldier snapped, still looking straight ahead.

"General?" mumbled Jeff. "Mom's a general?"

"Wait a second," Holly said to the guard.

"How did you know his mother's name is Margaret Ryan?"

The guard frowned. "I . . . I made that up," he said. "Besides there are no such things as aliens."

"Who said anything about aliens?" snapped Holly.

Jeff read a patch on the soldier's shoulder. "And why does your patch say *Alien Patrol Squad?*"

The soldier looked down at the patch. "Uh . . . my . . . uh . . . grandmother sewed that for me. Yes, that's right, my grandmother. Now you'd better go home and . . . play . . . or something."

"Look, an alien!" yelled Holly, pointing over the guard's shoulder.

"Green or blue?" the soldier cried, running off into the rocks with his gun lowered.

Before he had a chance to look back, Holly and Jeff dashed through the gate and ducked down next to a large airplane hangar.

What they saw was incredible. An army base full of tanks and trucks and Jeeps. Lots of soldiers marched here and there. But there was something else, too.

A shiny black helicopter stood outside a large building built right into the hillside.

Stenciled on the ground in front of the helicopter was a name. *General Margaret P. Ryan.*

"Your mom's parking spot," said Holly.

A moment later, they were in a hallway inside the large building. Dozens of other hallways shot off the main one like a spider's web.

"Just like some TV spy show," Jeff huffed, looking left and right for some clue about which way to go.

"I'm amazed we got this far," Holly whispered. "They're going to stop us before we ever get to your mom." She tugged Jeff's shirtsleeve. "And don't you dare tell me she works in a shoe store."

Jeff nodded. "I guess I can't believe that anymore."

Then he stopped. On the wall ahead of him was a sign that made him blink twice. "Holly? Does this say what I think it says?"

Holly read the sign over his shoulder.

Project S.H.O.E.S.T.O.R.E.
Special Head Office for
Extra-Super-Terrestrial
Organisms to Research and Examine

Jeff turned to Holly. A big smile spread across his face. "My mom doesn't lie!"

Holly rolled her eyes. "Yeah, well . . ."

They turned the corner and stopped.

There was a huge iron door blocking the hallway. It had no doorknob or handle. A small gray box was on the wall next to it.

The box spoke in a robotic voice. "Password?"

Jeff looked at Holly. She made a face and shrugged. "Say something pass-wordy."

"Um . . . shoe store?" Jeff said to the box.

"Incorrect!" droned the voice. "Pass-word?"

"Try your name," whispered Holly.

"Um . . . um . . . um . . ." Jeff stammered.

"Incorrect!" the box said. "Third and final try before alarm sequence begins. Password?"

"Come on, think!" Holly whispered. "Re-member the alien invasion! Hurry!"

Jeff couldn't think. No words came into his head. Not a single one, not even his own name. Time was running out. He was sweating. His breakfast began to churn in his stomach.

"Password?" the voice repeated.

Holly jumped up and down and started to push him from behind.

Jeff looked at her. He froze. His brain was a total blank.

Holly's eyes went wide. *"Jeffffffffffff!"*

The word echoed down the shiny hallway.

"Thank you!" said the little box.

The door slid open.

Holly and Jeff stepped into a large round room. The door closed behind them.

They were alone.

In the middle of the room was a metal stand about four feet high. A bright light shone down on it from the ceiling.

Lying on the stand, in the center of the spotlight, like a window display at the mall, were —

"Sneakers?" said Holly, walking over. "Oh, great. We risked our lives for a couple of pairs of junky old sneakers. Some guards must have left them. They probably stink, too."

"No way," said Jeff. But stinky sneakers

are what they looked like to him, too. Purple ones with yellow stripes on the sides and black soles.

"No way," Jeff said again, not believing they could only be sneakers. He moved closer. "They must be some kind of top secret space shoes."

"Oh, sure, top secret shoes," said Holly. "The secret is, why are they here? Come on, let's find your mom. Those clouds, remember?"

"Just a second." Jeff plunked himself down on the floor and pulled off his skates. "Ahhhh!"

"What are you doing?"

"Changing," Jeff said, rubbing his toes. "I can't move another inch in these skates. Besides, the sneaks will help us on the way down the hill. We'll get to town faster."

Holly looked at Jeff and shrugged. "I guess."

Jeff reached over and pulled both pairs of purple sneakers off the stand. He put one pair on.

Holly put on the other. "They actually fit."

"Uh-oh," mumbled Jeff. "I just remembered a movie where the guy takes something off a stand and the stand goes down and — "

VRRRRR! The stand slid down and disappeared into the floor.

" — and there were these loud alarms and — "

Weeeeeep! Weeeeeep! Weeeeeep!

"Alarms!" cried Holly. "Let's get out of here!"

"Wait," cried Jeff. "The laces!"

"Jefffffffffffffff!" screamed Holly.

"Thank you!" droned the voice at the door.

Fwing! The door slid open and the two kids shot down the long hallway.

Weeeeeep! Weeeeeep! The alarms howled loudly through the building.

"My mom's going to kill me for borrowing some super-top-secret stuff!" cried Jeff.

But Holly pulled him through the main

hallway and they jumped through the front doors just as they were sliding shut. A moment later, they were outside.

Alarms whined wildly across the hillside.

Floodlights from the watchtowers whipped back and forth across the grounds. Armed guards scrambled everywhere.

The two kids bolted along the building wall. When no one was looking, they leaped up over the fence and jumped down the other side.

The gate flashed open and dozens of soldiers swept down the hillside in the other direction.

"I think we lost them," whispered Jeff, crouching with Holly behind a ridge of rocks. "We're safe!"

Holly poked her head up next to him. "Yeah, but big deal. All we got out of it is sneakers!"

"I wonder what powers these things

have," Jeff mumbled, glancing down at the shiny yellow stripes running along the sides.

"You wear them and you run faster," Holly said. "And we'd better use them now. Look!"

Jeff turned to see the sky filling with dark clouds. Lots of them. And they were moving into position overhead.

Grover's Mill was turning darker by the minute.

"The alien invaders!" cried Jeff. "Under the ground and in the sky. It's a total invasion sandwich!"

The ground beneath their feet rumbled and quaked. The two kids slid and scrambled and tumbled all the way back to town.

Jeff knew something big was going on under the ground. He also knew that in a few minutes they'd probably find out what it was.

Within minutes they were at the back

door of the pretty blue house on Mike's street.

Holly put her hand on the doorknob and turned it.

The door creaked and they stepped in. Jeff felt shivers stab his back and neck. Slowly he opened the basement door and started down the steps. Holly was right behind him.

The cellar was empty. The floor that they had seen open before was still shut tight.

"Terrific!" groaned Holly. "Our friends are down there but we can't get to them!"

Jeff stepped up to the square plate on the wall. "That guy put his face on this thing and the floor opened. Maybe if you do that thing with the fingers on your nose? And then touch this?"

Holly gave him a look. "I guess." She brought her fingers together and held them in front of her nose. She pushed her fingertips against the plate.

Eeeee! The floor silently slid aside.

Before them was a set of steps curving down into the dirt beneath the house.

Eerie red light shone from somewhere far below.

Jeff took a deep breath. "Come on, Holly. We're running out of time. Those clouds are getting closer every minute."

Holly looked at Jeff and nodded.

Slowly, they walked down the steps.

When Moles Sing

The steps curved down into a rough passageway. The walls were dimly lit with the red light flickering from up ahead.

The passage seemed to go on forever.

"I don't think my house has this kind of tunnel thing under it," said Jeff.

"You hope it doesn't," said Holly. "But maybe it does now. Maybe all of our houses do. The way the ground has been shaking and quaking, who knows what these guys are doing down here?"

Jeff didn't like the thought of that. A word kept coming back to him. *Invasion.* What did it mean when aliens invaded?

What exactly would happen? Would he know what to do? Would he get to keep his stuff?

As they tiptoed along, the passage widened. Their steps took them further and further, winding downward from the surface.

They could see plumbing and sewer pipes and underground wires dangling from above.

Soon they began to hear strange sounds echoing up from below. Grinding and clanking. The rough walls hummed and rumbled.

"I feel like we're in some kind of giant blender," said Holly, touching the shaking walls to keep her balance.

"Yeah," said Jeff. "I just hope we're not, like, the stuff inside the blender that gets all goopy."

"Uh, right," Holly agreed.

They turned a corner and the sound was louder and clearer.

Boom! Chank! Boom! Chank! The clunking rhythm pounded through the tunnels.

And then, they heard something else.

The sound of feet scraping the rocky floor of the passage. And the sound of voices, echoing.

Holly yanked Jeff back into the shadows.

About twenty hooded creatures marched through the tunnel. The chief mole guy, Exetor, was leading them through the passage.

He was also leading them in song.

Their song was perfectly in time with the clanking from below.

Zoll! (boom-chank!)
Zoll! (boom-chank!)
Zoll! is zoomin' to our base.
He brings doom from outer space.
He'll entomb the human race.
He wants room in this weird place.
Zoll! (boom-chank!)
Zoll! (boom-chank!)
Zoll! He's zoominnnnnnnnn'!

Just as the creatures passed by the place where Jeff and Holly were hiding, they stopped. The creatures bobbed their heads here and there. Their little whiskers twitched in the air!

"They're sniffing!" Jeff hissed, pulling back.

Holly flattened against the wall, cupping her hand on her mouth.

Exetor peered into the darkness and sniffed. "Come, furry ones. Zoll will be here in the twitch of a whisker!"

A moment later, the creatures thumped by, their robes swaying to the clanging from below.

Zoll! (boom-chank!)
Zoll! (boom-chank!)

Then they were gone.

"That was way too close," Jeff finally said.

Holly nodded. "You're telling me? If they find us, they'll shoot us and kill us!"

"I don't think so," said Jeff, looking down the tunnel. "They're aliens. So they'll probably just vaporize us."

Holly made a face. "Oh, I feel a lot better, thanks."

"Let's follow them," Jeff said. "Down there."

Holly looked into the dim tunnel ahead of them. She breathed in deeply. "I am *so* not looking forward to this."

Jeff crept down the tunnel, hanging a left into another passage. The tunnel opened up onto a wide ledge. Jeff stopped at the end and looked down. Holly moved up next to him.

The sound was incredible.

Booming! Clanging!

But more than that.

Beneath them, in the rocks, was —

"A city!" gasped Holly.

Jeff nodded slowly. "Totally underground!"

It was a city and it was underground. Cut out of the rock beneath Grover's Mill were buildings and tunnels and towers. A city of many levels, circling around and around in a giant cavern.

"Well, somebody's been busy," Holly said.

Somebody was still busy. Dozens of hooded creatures scurried around on the different levels. And in what seemed like the center of the city was a flat area with a large X painted on it.

Jeff looked up. He could see the underside of the blue house. It was exactly above the X.

"Whoa!" gasped Jeff. "How much you want to bet that this guy Zoll is going to land his spaceship right there!" Jeff stared at the amazing scene. "What is this place?"

"Zoll Base One?" grumbled a voice.

"Good name!" mumbled Jeff, gazing down at the scene below. "But, why do you call it that, Holly?"

"I . . . I . . . didn't," Holly answered. "He did."

Jeff turned.

Holly's face was pale, her eyes wide with fear.

On either side of her were hooded creatures, clutching her tightly by the arms.

And towering over them all was Exetor, head mole alien.

"I knew I smelled humans!" Exetor growled.

"Grok! Grok!" his band of hooded mole soldiers snorted.

Exetor smiled a smirky smile and removed his hood. It was then that Jeff and Holly finally saw the mole alien's face up close.

It was leathery and black and wrinkly with tiny red eyes pulsing out under a single fuzzy eyebrow. His long snout had little white whisker things twitching around on the end of it.

"Whoa!" said Holly, pulling back from the snout. "With a snorter like that, you can probably smell what we had for break-fast!"

"Wheat-O cereal!" the creature grunted at Holly. Then his whiskers twitched some more. "With sliced banana and two-percent milk!"

Holly nodded, her eyes wide with wonder. "Exactly right!" She slid a stick of gum out of her pocket and started chewing it. "It's embarrassing."

"Of course it is!" the creature growled. "It's always embarrassing when you are face-to-face with a superior being!"

"Nose-to-nose," Jeff muttered to himself.

Then the mole alien raised his giant paws. They were a cross between little shovels and furry brown mittens.

"I am Exetor," he said. "Project Leader of Zoll Base One." His voice sounded hollow and deep.

"Uh, sure," said Jeff. "And you live down here?"

"Seven hundred of us," Exetor explained. "For the last week we've been digging under your town. Digging and building what you see here!" He pointed his paws at the city around them.

"That explains the manhole covers popping," said Jeff.

"And the rumbling below the streets," added Holly. "And the bumps, and sewer problems, and every other creepy thing that's been happening in Grover's Mill!"

"All part of our glorious invasion!" snorted one of the mole creatures behind Exetor. "When Zoll comes in his cloud ship, he will lead us up through the sewers into your town!"

"How nice!" said Holly. "Do you always travel first class?"

"Oh, we'll conquer all the towns that way," the mole went on. "We'll take over the world, then the solar system, then the galaxy, then — "

"Enough!" shouted Exetor, lowering his eyebrow at the other mole. "Now the earthlings know too much. We must destroy them!"

"Whoa, time out!" gasped Jeff. "Hey, we already forgot your plan. Right, Holly?"

"Forgot what?" said Holly, forcing a laugh. "See, we don't know anything about your plan! I mean, what plan? We don't know anything about a plan. Or anything!"

"Right," added Jeff. "So, we'll just grab our friends and go."

"Friends?" Exetor snorted with disgust. "You mean . . . *these?*" He moved a giant lever, and — *vrrrrt!* — the ground opened.

"Oh, no!" Holly gasped when she saw them.

Up from the center of the floor rose four large glass tubes. They turned slowly on a round platform. One of the tubes was empty. The other three had people in them.

"Liz!" cried Holly. She ran over with Jeff.

But their friends stood perfectly still in the tubes.

"Are they . . . dead?" gasped Jeff.

"Merely asleep," replied Exetor. "As you soon will be. And when mighty Zoll comes — "

Holly couldn't take it. She whirled around. "Listen, mole nose! You think you're going to invade? You think you're going to take over? Well, let me tell you about Grover's Mill! It's filled with kids like us who will fight for our freedom and the freedom of our friends and families!"

"Nice speech," smirked Exetor. "But you are all prisoners! Prisoners of the mighty Zoll!"

"Zoll!" repeated the others, slapping their hooded heads hard with their shovel paws. Then they slowly began to close in on the two kids.

Jeff got boiling mad, too. "Hold on, there, bathrobe boys! Just who is this guy *Zoll*, anyway?"

The moles froze in their tracks. They all looked at Exetor. Their snout whiskers twitched under their hoods.

The leader's furry eyebrow shot up. "Zoll?" he gasped. A quizzical look wrinkled across his leathery face. "Why . . . Zoll is Zoll!"

He stopped, as if that answer was enough.

"Zoll is Zoll, huh?" said Holly. "Well, thanks a bunch for clearing that up."

Exetor strolled over to the one empty tube. Then he stood back, folded his arms, and smiled. "You see, in the universe there are four things: solid, liquid, gas, and Zoll."

"Uh-huh." Jeff chewed his lip. "And where do we fit in?"

The mole's snout whiskers flicked up and down. *"You fit into this glass tube!"*

What's That You're Wearing?

An instant later, a hatch on the empty tube popped open. A bunch of mole aliens grabbed Jeff and threw him in. Then they came for Holly.

"Get your paws off me, you, you — moles!" she cried, trying to get free. But the moles held tight.

"We're short on Earthling Destruction Tubes," said Exetor. "You don't mind sharing, do you?"

"We do, actually," said Holly, still struggling. "That's something you gotta learn about earthlings. We have to have our own tubes. Sorry, I'll wait for the next one."

"OH, JUST GET IN!" Exetor shouted.

The mole aliens snorted and tossed Holly into the tube with Jeff. Then Exetor pressed a button on the outside of the tube.

Ssss! A stream of pink gas shot into the tube.

"Holly!" cried Jeff. "The sleeping gas!"

Before Jeff could think another thought, Holly spat out her bubble gum and slapped it over the nozzle. The gas stopped.

"Whoa! Quick thinking, Holly!" said Jeff.

"Oh, big deal," snorted Exetor. "Zoll can destroy you himself." Then he and his mole aliens scurried over to a giant control panel near the landing area.

"Don't worry, Holly," said Jeff. "We'll get out of here. We'll save our friends. We'll stop the invasion. We'll be heroes."

"Sounds great, Jeff," said Holly. "How?"

Jeff didn't answer right away. Mostly because he had absolutely no idea *how*. Not a clue. But it felt better to pretend that he did. "Can't tell you, not in front of them."

Holly nodded. "A secret plan! That's cool."

Yeah, right, thought Jeff. So secret even *he* didn't know it. It would take a miracle to get them out of this one.

Jeff tapped on the tube. "Hey, Mr. Mole. Why are you invading here? I mean, why attack our town?"

Exetor smirked again. "Simple. We needed a place where no one would notice us!"

Jeff instantly remembered the faces of Principal Bell and Mrs. Vickers when he and Holly told them about the aliens. "He's got a point."

The moles continued to work. They turned dials, moved levers. Some were checking screens with little green lights blinking on them.

Holly tried to stare a hole in Exetor's back. Then she turned to Jeff. "Oh, I wish this were one of my dad's movies. Then I could just walk out when it came to this part."

Jeff glanced around the cavern. The whole situation didn't look good. Their tube was sealed up tight. Their friends were taking a deep snooze. The control panels all around them were groaning and whining. The mole aliens were grunting.

And soon this guy Zoll would come and lead his stupid invasion!

Invasion.

The word sounded horrible. Scary. Grover's Mill taken over by mole aliens. Ugly mole aliens. Who would stop them? Who *could* stop them?

Jeff swallowed hard. "Hey!" he called out. "Why does Zoll hate earthlings?"

Exetor smirked. "Why? Because Zoll is Zoll!"

"Again with the Zoll-is-Zoll thing," said Holly, very annoyed.

"Silence!" shrieked Exetor. "He is coming!"

VRMMMM! Suddenly, the ground above them rumbled. Thunder boomed in the cavern.

"Open the landing port!" Exetor cried.

VRRRRT! High above them, the foundation of the pretty blue house slid aside, the roof of the house opened, and a giant cloud lowered itself through the house.

"Whoa!" cried Holly. "Even in The Weird Zone this is weird!"

Exetor raised his furry paws high above him and proclaimed, "To the glory of — Zoll!"

The cavern suddenly exploded in a burst of incredible bright light! A white cloud swirled down, filling the air.

"The invasion force!" gasped Jeff. "This is it!" He was scared, and angry. There were just seconds left! "Holly, we've got to get out of here!"

As the air turned misty and foggy, Jeff began kicking at the hatch door with his new sneakers. "I'll get us out of here if it's the last thing I — whoa!"

"Um . . . Jeff?" Holly said.

Something was going on with Jeff.

Jeff was . . . changing. Well, his feet were!

Thwonk! Flang! Chank-choonk! Grink! Jong!

The sneakers started to grow! Coiling up from the top of each sneaker was some kind of liquid metal stuff that covered Jeff's legs and went solid in an instant.

"Jeff," cried Holly. "What are you doing?"

But the sneakers weren't finished.

Flang! Glanch! Plung! Long, thick pieces of metal shot up from his waist, met across his chest, and coiled down his arms.

"I can't stop it!" Jeff yelled. "It's going by itself!"

Fwink-fwank-fwunk! A chunk of gray metal slithered up his chin and shot over his head, forming a giant spiked helmet.

By this time, the whole cavern was filled with fog.

And there stood Jeff. In the glass tube. Wearing a total armored suit!

He turned his head easily and said

through a grille over his mouth, "Bet you can't buy these in just any shoe store!"

Holly nodded slowly. "Uh-huh. Now, how exactly did you do that?"

Jeff tapped the tips of Holly's sneakers.

Thwonk! Flang! Chank-choonk! Grink! Jong!

A moment later, there were two of them.

"Cool suits," said Jeff, opening and closing his iron hands. "Suddenly, I don't feel so helpless anymore. What do you say we rescue our friends?"

"Let's do it!" said Holly.

But before they could do anything, the underground world exploded with a rainbow of jagged light.

Zoll had landed!

KLA-BLAMMO!

An enormous explosion of white, purple, green, and orange light filled the underground cavern!

The light faded to reveal a large, silvery cloud ship resting on the loading area.

VRRR! The ship opened. And he, Zoll, the great one himself, appeared on the platform in the center of the giant underground city.

Holly nudged Jeff with her armored elbow and whispered. "He's . . . tiny!"

It was true. Zoll was much smaller than the other mole aliens. His fur was light brown. He looked like a kid mole. But he wore big chunky blue boots and swirled a long silver cape.

"I'm Zoll, don't ya know!" he proclaimed to everyone in a high voice. "I'm wondrous! I'm all sparkly in my cape! And I'm cute!" Then his mole whiskers flicked out and he growled in a lower voice. "And I wanna take over the world!"

Then Zoll pointed to his feet. "Like the boots? They're new!"

Exetor and the moles bowed before Zoll and began swatting their heads.

Jeff nudged Holly and whispered, "They haven't seen us yet!"

"Shall we introduce ourselves?" asked Holly.

"Yoohoo! Mole guys?" Jeff growled. "Take a look at us! We're metal — and we're mean!"

Exetor and his creatures looked up from the floor. It was as if their eyebrows hit the ceiling. Their red eyes bugged nearly all the way out. Their snout whiskers got all twitchy.

Zoll's eyes pulsed with rage. "Hey!" he shouted at Jeff and Holly. "Who are you two weird robots? Didn't anybody tell you that there are only four things in the universe — solid, liquid, gas, and me?"

"I told them!" cried Exetor.

The two kids popped the tube hatch open and jumped down like superheroes right into the middle of the mole guys.

"We're Jeff and Holly!" said Jeff, smiling in his helmet.

"We're Jeff and Holly!" Zoll repeated, snarling. "WELL, I'M ZOLL — AND I'M INVADING YOUR TOWN!" Then he growled and pulled something from under his cape. It was a jagged bolt of something pink. He hurled it at Jeff.

ZAM! It blasted like lightning on Jeff's spiky helmet!

Jeff shook his head. "Cool!" he said, laughing. "No pain at all!"

Then Holly held out her arm and suddenly — *zammmm!* — a bolt of blue energy from the tips of her fingers blasted the mole aliens.

"Also cool!" she said as the mole aliens dived to the ground. "I like the sneakers, but I *looooove* the accessories!"

Zoll hopped down from the platform and scurried over to Exetor. He had an angry look on his snout. "You were supposed to get everything ready! I brought my personal attack force in very spiffy cloud ships all the way from Zollkan — at snacktime, no less — and everything's *not* ready!" Zoll's voice was screechy.

"Destroy the enemies!" Exetor yelled out, pointing at Jeff and Holly.

"That's better!" mumbled Zoll. "I like the *destroy* part."

A pack of mole aliens rushed at the two kids.

ZAM! ZAM! Holly let another blast of blue laser stuff fly out from her metal fingers.

The moles jumped for cover.

Jeff turned to Holly and grinned. "Fancy shooting, partner! Now's our chance to save our friends. Let's go!"

The two super-robotic totally armored heroes leaped across the landing area to the three giant tubes. With incredible strength, they blasted open the hatches and pulled their friends out.

The three sleeping kids woke up, but they were groggy.

"Can't I have just one more?" Mike muttered, rubbing his eyes.

"I was *not* picking my nose," said Sean in a daze.

"It's spelled w-e-i-r-d," Liz mumbled sleepily.

Holly grinned at Jeff. "Our friends are back!"

"Friends!" screamed Zoll. "Zoll doesn't allow friends! And guess what? I'M ZOLL!"

ZWAMMO! The little lord of the moles hurled another pink bolt at Jeff and Holly. Then he plucked a little pink box off his belt and shouted into it. "Calling all cloud ships! Calling all cloud ships! BEGIN THE ATTACK — NOW!"

BLAAAAAAAAAAMMMMMMM!

The cavern rocked and thundered from an incredible blast! The cloud ships were attacking Grover's Mill!

The Battle for Our World

The giant underground city quaked and shook as the cloud ships began their attack from above.

"We'd better get up there!" said Holly, easily lifting Liz and Mike into the air.

Jeff tossed Sean over his shoulder and raised his other arm over his head. He jumped a little.

WHOOOOM! A small rocket on the back of his armored suit shot out a cool blue flame and Jeff soared thirty feet up the cavern.

A moment later, both armored friends were sweeping up to the surface.

"Hey!" yelled Mike, waking up on Holly's

shoulder. "Robots are flying us around!"

"Too bad," mumbled Liz, slumped over Holly's other shoulder. "That means we're still in The Weird Zone!"

The five kids blasted up through the blue house and out to street level.

There were dozens of cloud ships circling over Grover's Mill and blasting the ground below.

KLA-BAMM! KLA-BAMM! The ground shook and quaked with each explosion. A giant-sized bite of donut flew off the Donut Den and crashed to the ground.

"They're making a mess of our town!" cried Holly.

"And my lawn!" shrieked Mr. Sweeney as a horrible, screeching purple ray hit his yard, sending chunks of dirt and grass high in the air.

"Come on!" cried Jeff. "Let's get up there! We've got to do what we've got to do!"

Holly turned to him. "That's sort of like Zoll is Zoll, Jeff! But I think I know what you mean."

They set their friends down gently, and watched them run to Mike's house for safety.

Then, like human rockets, the two armored mole fighters shot off into the sky, each of them holding their arms out and flying straight for the circling alien spacecraft.

BLAMMM-O! Blast after blast shot from the clouds at the kids!

But the two friends put on their own awesome display of laser power!

ZANG! KEEOOW! Jeff and Holly zoomed in and out and between the giant spaceships, dodging their screeching rays and answering them blast for blast!

Suddenly, the clouds began to spin around and around. An instant later, they all merged into one huge cloud over Grover's Mill. The town grew dark.

"The big attack!" cried Jeff. "Let's blast that oversize cotton ball into orbit!"

Holly gave him the okay sign with her

metal fingers and shot off into the sky over Lake Lake.

Jeff soared high toward the cloud, then dropped into a steep dive to draw the ship's fire.

BLAM! BLAM! Bolts of purple lightning followed him. They missed, blowing a chunk of fin out of the fish-shaped Baits Motel.

Holly looped around the Grover's Mill water tower, skimmed low over the W. Reid Elementary School gym, and then cut back up toward the ship.

Then both at once, she and Jeff fired spray upon spray of red-hot laser rays directly at the heart of the cloud.

ZAM!—Z AM! — KA-BLAM!

The huge cloud rocked and shook and bucked and jerked and then was silent.

"Victory!" Jeff cried out loud. He glanced around. He was soaring hundreds of feet above Grover's Mill. His hometown looked like a little toy village below him. It seemed so helpless.

But now it was safe.

"This I can do!" Jeff cried out, smiling big.

Suddenly, something felt wrong. Jeff was losing power. He started to dip. He looked back at Holly. The blue flame on her suit started to sputter. She couldn't keep herself on course, either.

Jeff tried to jet over to her.

But he couldn't. "Holly, I'm — falling!"

Bong! The clock on the Double Dunk Donut Den chimed out.

And Jeff knew, as he and Holly fell hundreds of feet to the ground below, that their time was up!

All Cool Things Must End!

*J*ong! *Grink! Choonk-chank! Flang! Thwonk!* The incredible armor collapsed back into plain old purple sneakers.

"Uh-oh!" gasped Jeff, tumbling fast. "No more fancy suits!"

Holly tumbled next to him. Faster and faster! "Jeff, we're not going to make it!"

Suddenly, the huge pan on top of Usher's House of Pancakes let off a giant puff of steam!

SSSSSSSSSSSSSSS!

Jeff and Holly fell right into the puff and were lifted up on a pillow of soft billowy air! They were saved!

Slowly the steam faded into mist and

they tumbled gently into the huge pan.

Holly looked over. "Well, that was lucky!"

Jeff grinned. "Just like in the movies!" But all at once his grin turned to horror as he looked at the street below him.

WHOOM! A manhole cover burst in the air and a mole alien poked his head up from below.

WHOOM! Another manhole cover popped up. Then another and another!

And climbing out of the sewers just below Main Street was the evil mole kid himself, Zoll! He flashed his silver cape and stomped his big blue boots.

"Up, my mole army!" yelled Zoll. "Up from the sewers! Up — and conquer!"

"Oh, no! We're not finished yet!" shouted Holly. "It's the — ugly alien mole invader himself!"

"And, guess what?" screamed the whiny high voice of Zoll. "You can't stop me — now that you're just — plain old earthlings!"

"There's no such thing as plain old earthlings!" Holly screamed back. She and Jeff quickly jumped from the giant pan and climbed down the side of the House of Pancakes to Main Street.

They froze in horror as they saw hundreds and hundreds of hooded mole heads poking up from the sewers below.

"What are we going to do now?" gasped Jeff. "This is hopeless!"

"We've got to stop them!" cried Holly.

"But we're not robots anymore. Just kids."

Holly looked at Jeff. . . . "That's gotta be enough."

WHOOM! More manhole covers exploded. And from each one a mole head popped up and looked around.

Then Jeff's heart leaped as he saw three figures appear on Main Street behind the moles. They were holding long sticks and gliding fast.

"Sean?" said Jeff. "Mike? Liz?"

"Yes!" cried Holly. "Reinforcements!"

The three skaters barreled up the street and slid to a stop in front of Jeff and Holly. Sean held out two sticks to them.

He pointed over his shoulder at the mole aliens. "Looks like we've got a game to finish."

Holly nodded. "The game of our lives."

Liz nodded at her and smiled.

Mike crouched and made an ugly face at the moles.

"Let's play ball!" yelled Jeff. "I mean — puck! I mean — moles!"

The five friends drove hard down the street, slapping at the mole aliens wherever their twitching whiskers popped up!

Thwang! — grok!

Fwunk! — grok!

Slappp! — grok!

It was incredible to see. Up one street and down another, the five friends drove the moles back underground. Every time a mole head popped up — THWACK! — it got a hockey stick to the side of its furry head!

"They like to swat their own heads," cried Holly, dashing at another mole. "They ought to *loooove* this!"

While all this was going on Zoll was stomping up and down in his big blue boots and getting madder by the minute. "I don't like these people!" he growled at Exetor, who stood behind him holding a pile of Zoll's pink lightning bolts. "Oh, give me some of those!"

Zoll grabbed several bolts and starting heaving them at the five kids.

ZAM! ZAM! ZAM! the bolts exploded.

But Sean, Holly, Jeff, Mike, and Liz dodged them all and kept coming.

"We're kids!" shouted Sean.

"Grover's Mill kids!" cried Liz.

"Earthlings!" yelled Jeff.

"But — I AM ZOLL!" Zoll shrieked. Then his little mole chin began to quiver. "Oh, everyone to the ship! They don't play fair! I wanna go home! Maybe it's still snack time!"

A few seconds later — *VROOOOOOOM!*

Zoll's cloud ship rose up from the roof of the pretty blue house and settled over Main Street. The street filled with fog.

Zoll, and Exetor, and all the mole aliens disappeared into it.

"Home! And make it snappy!" mighty Zoll screamed.

A second later, the little cloud ship joined the big cloud ship. The big ship flashed red and shot swiftly over the mountains. Soon there was nothing but blue sky.

It was sunny in every direction.

A regular, normal Saturday afternoon.

"Grover's Mill, one," said Jeff. "Mole aliens, zero!"

Holly turned to Jeff. "So I guess maybe hockey *is* your game!"

The kids laughed and turned toward Mike's house.

Suddenly — *THONKA! THONKA!*

The swirling blades of a shiny black helicopter whizzed above them. Dust blew up everywhere. A figure in a military uniform jumped down from a ladder.

"Hi, Mom!" yelled Jeff.

Mrs. Ryan strode over and gave Jeff a tight smile. She held out two pairs of hockey skates. "Kids, I think you have something that doesn't belong to you."

Jeff slumped his shoulders. He sat on the curb and pulled off the purple sneakers. Holly did the same.

"These really are awesome sneaks, General," said Holly.

"General?" Mrs. Ryan looked startled. "You must mean general *manager*. Everyone knows I work in a shoe store!" But a moment later, she was climbing up the ladder to the chopper and heading back off into the hills.

Jeff turned to Holly. "Hey, I gotta believe her."

"Excuse me, Jeff," said Liz. "You still believe that whole shoe store thing? I mean, why?"

"Why?" repeated Jeff. "Because I am I!"

"No," said Holly. "*I* am *I*!"

"Uh-uh, I said it first!" Jeff protested.

"Yeah, but still!" said Holly.

Sean, Liz, and Mike gave their two friends a weird look as —

Bong! the giant donut chimed.

Sssss! the huge pancake pan hissed.